THE
BOARDWALK

THE BOARDWALK

REED FARREL COLEMAN

RAVEN BOOKS
an imprint of
ORCA BOOK PUBLISHERS

Library and Archives Canada Cataloguing in Publication

Coleman, Reed Farrel, 1956–, author
The boardwalk / Reed Farrel Coleman.
(Rapid Reads)

Issued also in print and electronic formats.
ISBN 978-1-4598-0674-0 (pbk.).—ISBN 978-1-4598-0675-7 (pdf).—
ISBN 978-1-4598-0676-4 (epub)

I. Title. II. Series: Rapid reads
PS3553.O47443B63 2015   813'.54   C2014-906596-5
C2014-906597-3

First published in the United States, 2015
Library of Congress Control Number: 2014951594

Summary: In this murder mystery, the death of an NYPD officer leads PI
Gulliver Dowd closer to the truth about his sister's murder. (RL 3.0)

*Orca Book Publishers is dedicated to preserving the environment and has
printed this book on Forest Stewardship Council® certified paper.*

Orca Book Publishers gratefully acknowledges the support for
its publishing programs provided by the following agencies:
the Government of Canada through the Canada Book Fund and the
Canada Council for the Arts, and the Province of British Columbia
through the BC Arts Council and the Book Publishing Tax Credit.

Cover design by Jenn Playford
Cover photography by Getty Images

ORCA BOOK PUBLISHERS   ORCA BOOK PUBLISHERS
PO Box 5626, Stn. B   PO Box 468
Victoria, BC Canada   Custer, WA USA
V8R 6S4   98240-0468

www.orcabook.com
Printed and bound in Canada.

18 17 16 15 • 4 3 2 1

For Bea and Herb

ONE

Gulliver Dowd was waiting in his Red Hook loft for his new office furniture to arrive. He no longer lived in the loft. He kept some space for his business—Gulliver Dowd Investigations, Inc. He rented out the rest of the loft to a group of young artists. He liked artists because they could create new worlds. They could shape those worlds to match the ideas in their heads. Their work could inspire people. All Gullie inspired people to do was to point at him. To laugh. To whisper and stare.

The loft in Red Hook had once belonged to his sister, Keisha. Loyal. Loving. Fierce. A warrior. The best sister ever. She was dark-skinned. A bit heavy. Even more unwanted than Gullie. Before his parents adopted her, she had been passed from one foster home to another. The things she told him about how she was mistreated in those homes made Gullie mad. Made him feel less sorry for himself. Because of his misshapen body and his lack of height, he had been teased. Bullied. Pitied. But he had never had to put up with what Keisha had to deal with. No one had ever forced themselves on him. No one took a strap to him. No one beat him until his bones broke. All those things had been done to Keisha. Worse. Yet Keisha had overcome.

She'd made it through high school. Suffolk County Community College. The New York City Police Department Academy. That's right. Keisha had become a member of the NYPD. The day she graduated was the proudest day of her life. It was the proudest day of Gulliver's too. He loved the pictures they took that day. They were so happy. The two runts nobody wanted. The dwarf and the abused black girl. Those framed photos were the only things on the walls of his new office. When Keisha was found murdered behind a building in Brooklyn, Gulliver thought he would never stop crying. It felt like his heart had been cut out.

Yet Keisha's murder had given him a new life. It had made him overcome too. When the cops couldn't find her killer, Gulliver decided he would do what they could not. He would find Keisha's killer. Bring him to justice. Avenge her murder. To that end, Gulliver had become a crack shot. A black belt in jujitsu. An expert with knives. He'd gotten his private investigator's license. He would never have believed it possible. Not any of it. He had been laughed at for so long, he had believed he was worthless. But in Keisha's death, he found himself. He found worth. He found purpose. But he had yet to come close to finding her killer. No one had.

Gulliver had lived in the loft since Keisha's murder. He felt close to her there. It helped keep her memory alive in him. He had come to love Red Hook. Red Hook had once been the toughest place in Brooklyn. In all of New York City. That was really saying something. Those days had passed. Now it was a hip place to live. It had a Fairway Supermarket. An Ikea! Tapas bars replaced topless bars. But it was still rough around the edges. Keisha had liked that about Red Hook. Gulliver too. Gullie's girlfriend, Mia, did not like it so much. She had her reasons. So they had moved to the other side of Brooklyn. Keisha would have understood.

Gullie looked at his watch. He wasn't worried about the furniture. He knew that it might not be delivered for two more hours. He was more worried about lunch. His friend Sam Patrick had promised to keep him company while he waited. To bring turkey hero sandwiches from their favorite deli. And a six-pack. Sam was an NYPD detective at the 76th Precinct. Red Hook's precinct. But neither Sam nor lunch was anywhere in sight. Gulliver was getting hungry. Impatient too. Worse, he was bored. So bored he was about to knock on the artists' door. He liked looking at their work. Just as he raised his hand to knock, the phone rang.

"Gulliver Dowd," he answered.

"Dowd. You hungry yet?" It was Sam Patrick. His voice was strained.

"Even little bellies get empty. I'm starving. Where the hell are you?"

"Sorry, Dowd, but I can't make it over today." Sam had a coughing fit. Then said, "Something's come up. Something I didn't see coming. I've got some things to put in order." He coughed again.

"You got a chest cold?"

Sam laughed. "Something like that."

"This business you got. You want to talk about it?" Gullie asked. "I got nothing to do until the furniture gets here. Might as well yak to keep my mind off being so hungry."

"Sorry, pal. No time for that."

"Is it police business, Sam? You can tell me."

Sam coughed again. "Bigger than that. We can talk about it later."

"Later?"

"Yeah. We need to talk. Just you and me. Somewhere private."

"You can come here later," Gullie said. "Or you can come by the apartment. Mia is working a night shift at the vet clinic."

"No!" Sam shouted, coughing again. "Not anyplace near other people. Not an office. Not an apartment. Not a bar."

"Okay, Sam. Whatever you say."

"Dowd, I wouldn't ask if it wasn't important." Now it sounded like Sam Patrick was choking back tears.

"I said I would meet you, but I need to have an idea what this is about."

"Just take my word for it, Dowd. It's important. You need to hear what I've got to say."

"But about what?"

There was silence on Sam's end of the line. Dowd could almost hear Sam thinking. Gulliver didn't like guessing games. He didn't like surprises.

"I'm hanging up now," Gulliver said.

"Don't, Dowd! Please, don't!" He coughed some more.

"You're worrying me, Sam. Tell me what's going on. I can help."

"No, you can't. Not with this."

Gulliver really was worried now. "With what?"

"Promise me you'll meet me. Then I'll tell you."

"I give up. Okay. I promise to meet you."

Sam asked, "You know Plumb Beach?"

"Sure I do," Gullie said. "Off the Belt Parkway between Knapp Street and Flatbush Avenue."

"Meet me in the parking lot at eight."

"Plumb Beach parking lot. Eight," Gullie repeated. "Now tell me what this is about."

Sam coughed. Cleared his throat. Then said one word. "Keisha."

Gulliver shouted into the phone for Sam not to hang up. But Sam Patrick was already gone.

TWO

Gulliver and Mia's new apartment was not ten minutes from Plumb Beach. He checked his watch. Saw he had a few minutes before he had to leave to meet Sam. He decided to give Mia a call. He still couldn't believe how much he missed her when they weren't together.

"Hey, Gullie. I've only got a minute. Is everything okay?"

He didn't want to mention Keisha. Not yet. Not until he had met with Sam and found out what was going on. He also didn't want to lie to Mia.

"It's been a long day, and Sam's being a little mysterious. I guess I just needed to hear your voice."

"I like that. But are you sure you're okay?"

"With you in my life, how could anything be wrong?"

"Okay, I've got to go. I love you, Gulliver Dowd."

"I love you more, Mia."

"Wanna bet?"

Gullie smiled to himself. "What do I get if I lose?"

"You get to sleep with me," she said.

"And if I win?"

"You get to sleep with me."

"Okay," Gullie said, "it's a bet."

They hung up. Gullie checked his watch again. Time to go. He headed downstairs.

He got to their meeting spot in plenty of time. Sam Patrick had chosen well. Gulliver's van was alone in the parking lot.

And there wasn't much traffic on the road. Snow was in the air and in the weather forecast. Clouds hung close to the ground. The lights of Kingsborough Community College glowed rainbow colors in the distance. The waters of the Atlantic rolled to shore less than a hundred feet from the nose of Gullie's van. But Gulliver wasn't interested in the glowing lights. He wasn't listening to the pounding waves. He wasn't even thinking about his phone call with Mia. All he could focus on was what Sam had said about Keisha.

He had tried to get back in touch with Sam many times during the day. Phone calls to Sam's home number went unanswered. Calls to his cell phone went straight to voice mail. Gullie walked over to the 76th Precinct to talk to him. Sam wasn't there. Gullie had even driven to Sam's house. But Sam's car wasn't in the driveway. It wasn't in the garage. No one answered the front door.

Now Gulliver didn't know what to think. Didn't know what to feel. It was more that he was feeling many things at once. Hope. Excitement. Worry. Fear. Anger. A thousand things. He might get a break in Keisha's case at last. It had been so long. The trail had gone so cold. He had almost lost hope. But he was worried too. Sam had been so weird on the phone. His voice so strained. Coughing. Almost crying. Still, Gulliver was mad at Sam. He had always felt Sam knew more about Keisha's murder than he would tell.

Sam and Gulliver had run into each other over a year earlier. Sam had come to Gulliver's door to question him about the beating of a street kid. The street kid had hired Gulliver to find his missing dog. Long story. But Gulliver remembered Sam because he had worked with Keisha in the 75th Precinct. Sam Patrick was in uniform back then. Just like Keisha. Gullie remembered that Sam had been nice to

Keisha. He had come to the funeral and to the gravesite. Almost seven years had passed since the funeral and Sam coming to Gullie's door. They had become friends after that. Over the past year Gulliver had asked Sam many times about Keisha. About her murder. Each time, Sam steered their chat in another direction. Sam never really answered the questions. Maybe he was finally ready to tell what he knew. But why? And why now?

For the second time that day, Sam didn't show. This was strange. Sam had always kept his word. And it was Sam who had made such a big point about this meeting. Gulliver tried Sam's cell number. His house number. But it was just like before. All he got was voice mail. The answering machine. He left messages on both. There was nothing else to do but go home. Whatever Sam knew about Keisha's murder would have to wait.

Gulliver pulled out of his parking space. Built up speed and merged into the right lane of the Belt Parkway. There were almost no cars on the road. Snow was falling in big lazy flakes. He smiled in spite of his anger and worry. He liked to watch snow fall. He kept in the right-hand lane. Drove at fifty because he had to get off at the next exit to loop around toward home. Yet he felt uneasy. Something wasn't right. He didn't know how he knew it. He didn't know what it was. But it was out there. And all the pretty snow in the world couldn't change his mind.

That's what made Gulliver a good PI. He had a feel for the world beyond his five senses. He saw trouble coming around a corner before he saw the corner. He thought it was because he was built like a hound. Close to the ground. Mia sort of agreed. She said his lack of height let him take in the world the way a child does. Whatever the reason, he felt danger close by. And then there it was, in his side-view mirror. There was a van coming up on him fast. Its headlights switched off. Trying to hide itself in the darkness and snow. Almost before he could think, the van was on him.

Bang! It smashed into Gullie's rear wheel. He fought hard to control his van. It fishtailed. The back skidding hard right. Then hard left. Then back again. Gulliver got it under control. But just as he did— *bang!* The other van hit the same spot. This time much harder and at a sharper angle. Gulliver's van was fishtailing like crazy now. Even though Gulliver was small, the van had been custom built just for him. It was like a race car built around the driver. Still, Gulliver could only just get it back under control. The third hit was too much. When the other van slammed into Gullie again, he lost control. His van spun around twice. Hit the center guardrail. Slid back across all three lanes and flipped over onto the right shoulder. The other van vanished into the night.

Before Gulliver even opened his eyes, he felt snow on his face. He sensed people kneeling over him. Could feel their hands on him. Heard their voices.

A woman asked, "Is the kid all right? Did you get his parents out?"

"There were no parents," a man answered. "And he's not a kid. He's a dwarf."

"Little person," the woman corrected. "They don't call them dwarfs anymore."

If Gulliver's ribs weren't killing him, he might have laughed. He pretty much ached all over. His ribs and head more than the rest of him. As his eyes opened, he heard sirens in the distance. Gulliver propped himself up on his elbows. His van was a mess. It was tipped over on the passenger side. The front end was smashed up. The rear driver's-side wheel well was pushed in.

He saw that there were two other cars parked in front of his van. He noticed that the snow was no longer falling in big lazy flakes. Now it was coming down in steady sheets. There was almost an inch of it piled on the road and on the cars. He must have been out of it for a while. He got to a knee to stand.

"Stay down, buddy," the man said. "You might have some broken bones or something."

"Yeah," the woman agreed. "Stay down. The cops are coming. You're not breathing so good."

But Gulliver was nothing if not stubborn. You didn't get to where he had gotten without being tough. Without being stubborn. He got to his feet.

"Thanks, folks," he said. "It was brave of you both to stop to help me. Couldn't have been easy to get me out of there."

"I would want someone to help me," the man said.

The woman nodded.

Gulliver took a few steps. His legs wobbled. He fell back to his knees. Tried sucking in big gulps of air. But he felt faint. Then his world went black.

THREE

The air was warm against his skin. It no longer smelled like burnt rubber from skidding tires. Instead it smelled of pine-scented cleaner. Of bleach. Of alcohol. He tasted copper on his tongue, as if there was blood in the air. He was no longer in the snow. But the back of his clothes was still wet. His ribs were aching. His head pounding. His mouth dry. His throat like sandpaper.

When he opened his eyes, no one was kneeling over him. He was in a hospital. The ER. He knew the sights. Knew the smells.

19

Knew the sounds of a hospital. A curtain was drawn around the bed. There was a lot going on around him. On the other side of the curtain doctors were barking orders. Nurses were reading off numbers.

"We're losing him!" a doctor screamed. "Get him up to the OR. Stat!"

Feet were scurrying. Shuffling. Racing. A gurney was wheeled by the curtain. Gullie saw the shadows on the floor. Things got quiet for a moment. It was as if the person on the gurney had sucked all the air out of the room.

Then the curtain around him split open. A woman in powder-blue scrubs came in. She had a stethoscope around her neck. By normal standards, she was short. But she was taller than Mia and many inches taller than Gullie. She had a round face. Thick black hair. Almond-shaped eyes. Light brown skin.

"Hello, Mr. Dowd. I am Dr. Agbay."

"You're Filipino," he said.

She smiled. It was a smile to light up a room. "Very good. How did you know that?"

"In my business, you learn a lot about people. Sometimes too much. Where am I?"

"Coney Island Hospital."

"What was all the excitement about?" he asked.

The doctor's pretty smile vanished. She shook her head. "Terrible. Terrible. A policeman was shot on the boardwalk this evening. Terrible."

"Is he going to make it?"

She didn't answer. "Come, Mr. Dowd. Let us have a look at you."

The doctor examined Gullie.

"You have some bruised ribs. A mild concussion too. Some bruises. You will live. How do you feel?" Her smile returned.

"Like an elephant is sitting on my ribs. And someone is hitting my head with a baseball bat. I could use a drink of water."

She poured him a glass.

While he drank, she said, "We'll tape up those ribs. Get you some pills for your pain. Your head will feel better in a few days. The ribs will take longer. In two weeks you will be a new man."

"I wish."

They both laughed.

"I don't know," said Dr. Agbay. "You are a very handsome fellow."

He shook his head. He always felt his handsome face was more a curse than a blessing. God's little joke. His face made him stick out even more than his lack of height. More than his misshapen body. It made people pity him. In college, a pretty girl had looked at his handsome face and his ugly body. She said, "What a waste. What a waste." Those words haunted him.

"There is a policeman waiting for you," the doctor said. She taped Gullie up. She gave him some pain pills. "I will send him in."

"Thanks, Doc."

"You take care of yourself, Mr. Dowd."

The policeman who came in was tall. He had big shoulders. A hard face. He wore high black leather boots and a squashed-down hat. The markings of a highway-patrol cop. They had a bad rep. Even among other cops. They were the cops who didn't play well with others. The ones who didn't mind the blood and the bodies in car crashes. Gullie had dealt with many cops. Not with many highway-patrol types. He explained to the cop how another van had raced up on him. How it had rammed his van three times. How he had lost control. How he had woken up with people kneeling over him.

"Sounds about right," the cop said. "Matches the damage to your van. Too bad. Nice van."

"Custom built," Gullie said. "I hope I can get it fixed."

"Should be able to. Damage looks worse than it is. Believe me, I know what I'm talking about. I see lots of smashed cars."

"Thanks."

"It will be a while till you get it back," the cop said. "This is a criminal case now, so the van is evidence."

"I know."

"So, Mr. Dowd, I'm just taking your statement. The detectives will want to talk to you when you are up to it."

"I understand."

The cop leaned in close. "But just between us. Do you have enemies? Anyone who might want to run you off the road?"

Gullie laughed. Then grabbed his ribs. "If I didn't think so before, I do now."

"But why would a—I mean, why would you have enemies?"

"It's okay. You meant to ask why would a little runt like me have enemies?"

The cop turned bright red. "Sorry. Yeah."

"Hey, Napoleon had lots of enemies, right?

The cop laughed.

Then Gulliver said, "Believe it or not, I'm a licensed private investigator. That's why the ambulance crew found a knife and a SIG 9mm on me. I don't do divorce work. But PIs do make people mad sometimes. I guess I made somebody pretty mad."

"I was going to ask you about the knife and 9mm next," the cop said.

"Everything's in my wallet. You'll see I check out."

"Okay. I think I've got everything I need, Mr. Dowd."

"Officer, I couldn't help but hear the commotion before. My doctor told me a cop was shot on the boardwalk."

The cop shook his head. "Yeah. And it don't look good."

"I'm sorry," Gulliver said. "My sister was on the job. Killed in the line of duty."

"Really?"

Gullie raised his right hand. "That's not the kind of thing I would lie about. So what happened tonight?"

"Really bad," the cop said. "Accidental shooting. A patrol officer shot a detective during a chase on the boardwalk."

"What's the detective's name? I'll make a contribution to his recovery fund or send flowers to his wife."

"Patrick, I think. One of the guys says he worked out of the Seven-Six," the cop said. "Yeah, Sam Patrick. That's the guy."

Before Gulliver could even react, he heard the whispers outside his curtain.

"That detective died on the table. You better tell the other cops."

FOUR

Loss was Gulliver's worst nightmare.

He had been happy. But he feared happiness. Not the happiness itself. He was good with that. Being with Mia this past year was the best time of his life. Before her, he'd known only two happy months. Those were the two months he had dated Nina Morton as a senior in high school. When Nina turned her back on him, she took his joy with her. That was what he feared. Not that happiness was impossible to have. That it was impossible to keep. That happiness was like smoke. It was right there.

You could see it. Smell it. Taste it. Feel it. But you couldn't hold onto it. It was there. Then it was gone. Though he felt joy in his heart, someone or something could reach in and snatch it away.

Gulliver should have been used to having things taken away from him. Used to having no power over what was taken. Or when. Or why. His life was a history of loss. Things had been stolen from him even before he was out of the womb. And it only got worse after he was born. His real mother had removed herself from his life. She'd given him away when she saw what she had given birth to. Her baby was tiny. Deformed. Gulliver was the runt in a litter of one. Set adrift. Alone in the world.

Not much had changed since then. He was short. Very short. A dwarf. A little person. What did it matter what he was called? Labels didn't change things. Labels didn't soften the blows. Labels didn't restore what was taken. They wouldn't change the image staring back at him in the mirror. His head was too large for his body. His body too long for his legs. His legs too short. One shorter than the other. His arms too small. His hands and feet too big. Normalcy had been robbed from him the instant he was created. His distrust of the good things didn't stop there. The people taken from him hurt more than anything. His adoptive parents were both gone. Nina had ripped his heart out twice with her vanishing act. And, worst of all, Keisha. Now Sam.

As Gullie felt sorry for himself, that knot got tight in his belly. The highway-patrol cop had said Sam was killed in an accidental shooting. Was it an accident that Sam never showed at Gullie's office that day? That he never showed at Plumb Beach? Was it an accident that tonight someone had tried to run Gulliver off the road? The same night that Sam Patrick was killed. The same night Sam was going to finally tell the truth about what he knew of Keisha's murder. Gulliver didn't like it. He didn't like it one bit. He didn't believe it. And when Gulliver Dowd didn't believe something...watch out! He was going to find the truth. Bruised ribs and concussion be damned.

Gullie had tried to get right to it. The truth was like a fire lit under him. It sang to him. He could deal with the pain in his ribs. He could stand pain. A lot of pain. For most of his time on earth, he felt life was built out of pain. And the parts that weren't made of pain were made of loss. But the pain in his head wasn't like the sore ribs. For the first two days after Mia brought him home from the hospital, he could barely move. Or take bright light. Or almost any light at all. He couldn't read. Couldn't watch TV. Couldn't look at a computer screen. Even listening to the radio made his head want to explode. Then he would get sick to his stomach. He had had concussions before. He laughed at the term *mild concussion*. It was a stupid phrase. Like *minor surgery*. No such thing. For two days Gulliver Dowd stayed in the dark. Shut off from the world. Shut off from himself.

FIVE

By the time Gullie's head felt better, Sam Patrick's shooting death was already old news. It is the sad nature of our country that violence is too soon forgotten. There are always so many murders. Insane people with guns. Drive-by shootings. Terror bombings. What was the death of one cop in such a world? But it was also true that nothing in the modern world is ever gone. Once it's digital, it's forever. So it was easy for Gulliver to track down all the news stories on Sam's shooting. He had watched all the reports on the Internet. Some of the reports were done on the boardwalk close to where Sam had been shot. And not far from where Gullie and Mia now lived.

Mia had grown up near Detroit. She had always dreamed of living close to the ocean. So Gulliver made her dream come true. She had done the impossible for him. She had given him love. Made him a happy man. Giving her the Atlantic Ocean was the least he could do. He had purchased a condo on the top floor of an apartment building in Manhattan Beach. Far away from Red Hook. Far away from her bad memories of being kidnapped. Of nearly being murdered. From their apartment, they could see the board-walk. Beaches that stretched for miles to the east and west. The ocean. Blue-green water that seemed endless. Mia liked to joke that she could almost see Ireland on a clear day.

Manhattan Beach was next to Brighton Beach. Brighton Beach was next to Coney Island. They shared the same shoreline.

In the summer millions of people from all over New York City crowded these beaches. But in the gloom of winter the beaches were empty. Winter winds blew cold and strong off the Atlantic. As Gullie hobbled down the boardwalk, only a few old Russians and gulls kept an eye on him.

Yellow crime-scene tape blew in the wind near where Sam had been shot. A big splotch of his blood was still on the wooden boardwalk planks. Sam hadn't died there, alone in the cold. The thought of dying cold and alone made Gullie sad. It reminded him of how Keisha had been killed. Shot in the back of the head. Left to die alone in an empty lot behind empty buildings. At least Sam was in a warm place with people around him when he died. Does it really matter where you die? Whether you are alone or not? Sooner or later, we all find the answer to those questions. Sam found out sooner. Too soon.

The reports said that Sam was walking on the boardwalk. That a woman screamed for help. That Sam came running to help her. He had his weapon drawn as he ran to her aid. Another cop heard the woman's screams too. That cop was named Stevens. Officer Stevens was patrolling the board-walk. He was running too. But he was farther away from the woman than Sam was. What Stevens saw was a man with a gun in his hand running at a screaming woman. All the reports said that Stevens shouted for the man with the gun to stop. But the man didn't stop. He didn't say he was a detective. Stevens had no choice but to fire at the man.

Gulliver pictured it in his head. He imagined Sam running to help the woman. He imagined Officer Stevens running to help her too. Gullie saw how it could happen. It's sad but true that cops do sometimes shoot each other by accident.

Put people with loaded guns in dangerous spots and bad things can happen. Even trained people make mistakes. But Gulliver didn't believe this was an accident. Not for one second. There was no reason for Sam to have been on the boardwalk in a snowstorm. Sam didn't live near Coney Island. Coney Island wasn't even his precinct. He was supposed to be meeting Gulliver miles away from the boardwalk. It was a meeting Sam himself had set up. There were bigger reasons Gullie didn't believe it. The screaming woman was nowhere to be found. Calls for her to come forward had gone unanswered. And there were no witnesses. The story was Officer Stevens's story and his alone. With Sam Patrick dead, there was no one to prove Stevens a liar.

There would be an inquiry into the shooting. That was the law. Until then, it would be impossible to speak to Officer Stevens. Impossible for anyone except

Gulliver Dowd. He had his ways. Most of the time, his lack of height, his looks, did not work in his favor. But there were moments when his looks helped. People felt sorry for him. Or thought he was stupid. Or weak. Gullie was a good PI. Maybe a great one. He took pride in getting through doors that were shut to everybody else. That was for another day. Now he had to pay his respects to Sam's family.

SIX

Ahmed Foster was an ex–Navy Seal who had dated Keisha in high school. He and Gullie had met again at Keisha's funeral. Ahmed and Gulliver weren't exactly friends. Gullie had hired Ahmed to teach him knife fighting. Hand-to-hand combat styles they didn't teach you in dojos. Ahmed worked for Gulliver when he needed help on a case. Sometimes Ahmed just drove Gullie. Sometimes it was as simple as standing behind Gulliver and looking tough. Ahmed was African-American. Built like a linebacker. He had a way of staring at you that was scary. Gullie was a lot of things. Scary wasn't one of them. There were times when they worked together that Ahmed had to use all of his Navy Seal training. Like last year, when he'd helped Dowd rescue Mia from her kidnappers. All of Ahmed's skills were on display. Mostly, their dealings were about money. Until now. When Gulliver told Ahmed this case might also be about Keisha's murder, things changed.

"If this is about Keisha," Ahmed said on the phone, "your money's no good with me, little man."

Ahmed was one of only two people Gulliver let call him *little man*.

Gulliver got into the front seat of Ahmed's pearl-white Escalade. He was nearly frozen from standing on the boardwalk. Funny how he hadn't noticed he was so cold until he got into the warm SUV.

"Where to?"

"O'Malley's Funeral Home. You know it?"

"Coney Island Avenue and Avenue M."

"That's the one," Gulliver said. "When we get there, stay in the car."

"Whatever you say, little man."

* * *

O'Malley's was full of cops. A police honor guard stood on either side of Sam Patrick's casket. It was hard for Gullie to be there. It brought back all the horror of Keisha's murder. There had been an honor guard for her too. But her coffin was closed. The bullets had done terrible things to her face. Gullie had had to go to the morgue to identify her. It had taken months for him to get that image out of his head. Now it came rushing back to him. But he kept strong. He had to. For Sam's sake. For Keisha's too.

Some of the other cops were in uniform. Many were detectives. Gulliver knew most

of the detectives from the 76th Precinct.
He also knew a few from the 75th Precinct
where Keisha had worked. They all had sad
faces. Everyone did. Gullie nodded to them.
They nodded back at Gullie. He shook a
few hands. Walked to Sam's coffin. Gulliver
wasn't much on praying. He and God didn't
get along. So he just said goodbye to Sam.
He also promised his dead friend he would
find out what really happened.

He felt a tap on the shoulder. It was
Sam's ex-wife, Mary. Cops and marriage
don't always mix well. You can't be married
to two loves. Some cops love the job too
much. Sam was like that. The job won.
Mary and the kids lost. But Sam and Mary
had stayed close. Maybe because they
shared kids. Maybe because they still loved
each other. Gullie thought they did.

Mary was in her mid-forties. Her
reddish hair was going gray. She was still
pretty. Button-nosed. Blue-eyed. Today

those eyes were ringed in red. Her mascara had run from tears.

"Hi, Mary. So sorry about Sam. How are the boys holding up?"

"They're like Sam. Tough. I don't think it's hit them yet. Not really."

"Mary, can we talk?" Gullie asked.

"Sure."

Mary Patrick led Gulliver into a small room a few doors down from where the wake was. They were alone. They sat next to each other.

"What is it, Gulliver?"

"Do you believe this story about what happened to Sam on the boardwalk?" he asked.

She tilted her head. "Why wouldn't I? You knew Sam. If someone needed help, he helped."

"That was Sam. Do you know what he was doing on the boardwalk that night? He lived all the way over in Bay Ridge."

She shrugged her shoulders. "Who knows? Maybe he had a date. Maybe he just wanted to think. He liked to look out at the ocean when he had things on his mind."

"How was he lately, Mary? I was busy moving, and I hadn't seen him for a month or two. When I spoke to him on the phone the day he was killed, he sounded odd."

She nodded as if she agreed. "He was a bit strange over the last few weeks. We would make plans to see each other. Then he would back out at the last minute. Or he would show up at the house without calling first. He spent a lot of time with the boys over the last two weeks. I could tell something was going on with him. He didn't look well. He seemed jumpy. When I asked him about it, he wouldn't tell me. But he could be like that. He could keep secrets. It was one of the reasons I divorced him. He wouldn't tell me things."

"Did he ever talk about his time in the Seven-Five precinct? Did he ever talk about my sister?"

Mary's head sank. She put her hand on her heart. "Oh, Gullie," she said, "I forgot. Your sister was killed in the line of duty too. I'm so sorry. This must be terrible for you. It must bring it back."

He patted her arm. "It's okay, Mary. It's okay. But did Sam ever talk about Keisha?"

She shook her head. "No. He was pretty close-mouthed about his time at the Seven-Five. And if I ever mentioned your sister, he would get really mad. Now I have to get back inside."

"Again, Mary, I am so sorry for your loss," he said.

She didn't say another word. She just drifted out of the room.

Gulliver went back to the wake a few minutes later. He walked around the room. He shook some hands. But the one person he wanted to see wasn't there. He left. He decided that the answers he was looking for wouldn't be with the dead.

SEVEN

Just as he came out of the funeral home, a big hand thumped down on his shoulder. Gulliver looked up.

It was the man he had been looking for inside. Detective Ralph Rigo. Rigo had been Sam Patrick's partner for many years. They had been partners when Gullie and Sam became friends. A few months earlier, Rigo had gotten too rough with a suspect. That was Rigo's way. Fast with his fists. Slow with his brain. The NYPD had put Rigo on desk duty. Word on the street was that they were pushing him to quit. Rigo had tried to shove Gulliver around the first time they met. But Gullie had forced Rigo to his knees with a thumb lock. Since then, they had kept their distance from each other.

Rigo had been crying. His eyes were nearly as red as Mary Patrick's. He had also been drinking. His breath smelled of vodka. His sweat smelled of it. His clothes too. Rigo was a blob of a man with a big belly and a double chin. His time behind a desk had not helped him. He was even fatter now than he was when they met. Gulliver didn't like Rigo. Rigo didn't like Gulliver. But they both really cared about Sam Patrick.

"You believe that bullshit about the shooting?" Rigo asked Gullie.

"Not for a second."

Rigo's fleshy face lit up. He didn't believe it either.

"I keep telling people that it's crap," Rigo said. "But no one will listen to me. Why would Sam be on the boardwalk in the freakin' snow?"

Gulliver nodded. "I feel the same."

"Where's this mystery woman? She was screaming, but no one can find her. And no witnesses!"

"Forget that," Gullie said. "Sam called me that day. He was supposed to meet me at Plumb Beach at eight that night. So what was he doing on the boardwalk at all? You knew Sam. He would never do that. Just not show up. No. Somebody got him to the boardwalk."

"But who? And how? He wouldn't blow you off without calling," Rigo said, "unless he thought it was an emergency."

"Good questions. But there's more," Gulliver said. "When Sam didn't show the other night, a van ran me off the road. Nearly killed me."

"You think Sam's shooting and you getting run off the road are connected?" Rigo asked.

"Can't see how they're not."

Rigo agreed. "Makes sense. But why?"

"Another good question. I think it's got something to do with my sister's murder. Sam told me the reason he wanted to meet with me was about Keisha. Did he ever talk to you about that?"

"Never," Rigo said. "He didn't like talking about his time at the Seven-Five."

"That's just what his ex-wife said."

"Listen, Dowd, I want to help find out what went on with the shooting."

"Not if you keep drinking, Rigo. You're no help to me drunk. And you're no help to yourself."

"Okay, Dowd. No drinking."

They shook hands on it.

"First thing is, you have to stop telling people you don't believe what happened to Sam. We don't want to get too much unwanted attention. I know you like to go at things straight ahead. Not this time, Rigo. We have to be a little careful."

"Then what should I do?"

"We have to talk to the cop who shot Sam. Do you know anything about Stevens?"

"Sorry, Dowd. I don't know Stevens at all."

"All right. That's your job. Find out everything you can about Officer Stevens. Call in favors. Spread cash around if you have to. I can give you some if you need it."

"That's okay. I'll find out about him."

"How about finding out where he lives or where he's being stashed," Gullie said.

Rigo shook his head. "Forget it, Dowd. No one's going to tell me about that. The brass don't like these kinds of things. Until Stevens gets cleared of the shooting, he will be hard to see. I doubt his family even knows where he is."

"Let me worry about that, then. You find out what you can about Stevens."

They shook hands again. Gulliver watched Rigo walk away. It had begun to snow again. He turned up his coat collar. He hoped Ahmed had the heater going.

EIGHT

Mia was leaving for work as Gulliver got home. Mia was the head vet tech at an animal hospital in Sheepshead Bay. Gullie had met Mia when he was working his first and only missing-dog case. A street kid named Ellis Torres came up to Gullie at Valentino Pier in Red Hook. Ellis asked him to find his missing dog. The dog was named Ugly. When Gulliver found the dog, he saw that Ellis had given the dog the perfect name. Ugly was about the weirdest-looking dog he'd ever seen. As someone said, Ugly looked like a cross between a dog and an alien.

And the dog was pretty smelly too. So Gulliver took Ugly to the nearest vet clinic. Mia was on duty that day. Gulliver had been grateful to Ellis and Ugly ever since.

"How are your ribs?" Mia asked as she put on her coat.

"Sore, but better."

"When is Sam's funeral?"

"Friday."

"I'll come with you," she said.

"Thank you. I knew there was a reason I loved you."

She leaned over and kissed him hard on the mouth. "I hope there's more than one reason."

"After a kiss like that, I can think of a few hundred reasons."

She smiled that beautiful, shy smile of hers. "You and Ahmed make any headway?"

"Some," he said.

"That means you don't want to talk about it."

"There's one more reason I love you." He winked. "You know me so well."

"I've got to go." She leaned over and kissed him again. This time softly on the cheek.

"Love you."

After Mia had gone, Gulliver found himself staring out the window. He was trying to piece together what had really happened to Sam. But it was like trying to see the ocean through the snow and darkness. He knew the answers were out there somewhere. He just couldn't see them. One thing he was sure of. Keisha's murder was at the center of this somehow. One question kept going around in Gullie's head. Why did Sam want to talk about Keisha now? Gulliver figured if he could answer that question, he could answer all the others. The phone rang.

"Dowd here."

"It's Ralph Rigo."

"What you got for me?" Gullie asked.

"This guy Stevens. The cop who shot Sam. He's a real piece of shit. He makes me look like a Boy Scout."

"Only Attila the Hun could make you look like a Boy Scout."

Rigo wasn't laughing. "Very funny. For a midget freak, you got a big mouth."

"Sticks and stones, Rigo. Sticks and stones. Listen. We don't have to like each other. But we both want the same thing."

"To find out what happened to Sam," Rigo said.

"Right. So I won't bust your chops. You won't bust mine."

"Works for me. Like I was saying. Stevens is a badass. I think his Internal Affairs folder is two feet thick. I don't know how he's stayed on the job this long."

"How long is that?" Gulliver asked.

"Twenty years plus."

"And he's still a patrol officer?"

Rigo laughed. "Trust me. With his rep and record, he's lucky he's not a meter maid. Word is the Six-O in Coney Island is his last stop."

"So how *does* a guy like that stay on the job?" Gullie wondered aloud.

"He got a rabbi. Someone higher up who watches out for him. Someone with juice. With power."

"Like who?"

"Good question," Rigo said. "Good question. Maybe I'll try to find out."

"Do that. How about Stevens? Did you find out where he's at?"

"No luck, Dowd. No one I know has any idea where Stevens is. One guy who knows him says he's pretty sure he isn't home."

"Okay, Rigo. I'll try to call in a favor."

"I tried that."

"Not with the person I'm going to ask," Gullie said.

Rigo couldn't imagine that a little man like Dowd had connections. "Yeah. And who would that be?"

"Joey Vespucci."

There was a moment of silence. Then, "*The* Joey Vespucci? Joey 'Dollar Menu' Vespucci? The Mafia don?"

"No. Joey Vespucci who owns the fruit stand on Bay Parkway."

"How do you know the most powerful man in the Five Families?" Rigo's voice cracked.

"We took ballroom-dancing classes together."

"I thought we weren't going to bust each other's chops, Dowd."

"Sorry. You're right. I met Joey when I was working a case. He once offered help if I ever needed it. Now I need it. We need it."

"Good luck with that," Rigo said. "One more thing. I don't know if it means anything."

"What?"

"Stevens worked at the Seven-Five precinct at the same time as Sam and your sister."

"Maybe," Dowd said. "Maybe."

When he hung up the phone, Gulliver went back to staring out the window. He still couldn't see the ocean. He still couldn't see how the pieces in Sam Patrick's death puzzle fit together.

NINE

The media called him Joey "Dollar Menu" Vespucci. No one who knew him or feared him called him that. Few people knew him. Everybody feared him. When everyone else in the mob ran away from the spotlight like kitchen bugs, Joey stood under it. What Gulliver had found out was that the "Dollar Menu" thing was just part of a false image. It was make-believe. A mask. The real Joey Vespucci was a serious man. A deadly serious man. But he only showed that side of himself inside his home. To people he did business with.

Far away from the spotlight. Even the front of his house was part of the cheap image. The first time Gulliver saw the house, he thought it looked like a cross between a fast-food joint and a strip club. Just like the image he had of Joey. His opinion changed when he got through the front door.

Joey lived in the Todt Hill area of Staten Island. A favorite mob neighborhood. These days Joey was the only one left. The mob had been torn apart since the RICO Act was put into law. In the old days, no one ratted anybody out. These days mob guys flipped on each other at the speed of light. But Joey Vespucci was the last of his kind. Feared. Respected. Careful. Gulliver didn't think of Joey as a friend. He couldn't be friends with a man who had other people killed. And who had murdered people himself. But in the world of a PI, you can't always keep clean. You have to deal with the people in that world. Not with people you might pick and choose. You can't swim in dirty water without getting a little muddy yourself. Joey Vespucci was far from the worst person Gulliver had been forced to deal with. But he was the most powerful.

The last time Gulliver was here, he had Ahmed park around the corner. Not this time. This time Joey knew he was coming. Ahmed drove his Escalade right up to the front door. Gulliver told Ahmed to stay in the car.

"Trust me, Ahmed," said Dowd. "You would make all these guys jumpy."

"'Cause I'm black?"

"'Cause you look like you could kick their asses."

Ahmed nodded. "I can."

"That's the point."

Ahmed smiled.

Tony met Dowd on the front steps. Tony was Joey V.'s main muscle. A bodyguard. He was stout. He seemed to have no neck.

Tony and Dowd had history. Not a good history. On his first visit, Gulliver had got the better of Tony. He'd taken Tony's gun away from him. Tony wasn't happy to see Gullie then. He wasn't happy to see Gullie now. But Tony feared his boss more than he hated Gulliver.

"The boss is waiting for you, Bug," Tony said.

"Give it a rest, Tony. And maybe I won't take your gun away again."

As Gullie walked into the house, he heard Tony cursing to himself. He found Vespucci where he had the first time. Joey was seated behind a big fancy desk in his study. Gulliver wondered what Mafia dons studied. A broad smile lit up Joey's face when he saw Dowd. He stood up behind his desk. He came around and shook hands with Gulliver.

"Nice to see you again, little man." Joey Vespucci was the only person besides

Ahmed to call him that and get away with it. "You manage not to take Tony's toys away today?"

Gullie shook Joey's hand. "Tony and I played nice today. Good to see you too."

Vespucci motioned for Gulliver to sit. "Can I get you something to drink?"

"Vodka. The cheaper the better. On the rocks."

"Coming up."

Gullie watched Joey pour the drinks. Joey was a slender man in his mid-sixties. Handsome. With fiery brown eyes. His hair had gone silver. He handed Gullie his vodka. Joey had scotch. They clinked glasses. Then Joey sat down behind his desk.

"What can I do for you, little man?"

"You once said if I needed your help you would see what you could do."

Joey smiled again. "I remember. So you've come to ask a favor?"

"I would have asked last night on the phone," Gulliver said. "But I know you don't like talking business on the phone. And this is the kind of favor you ask face to face."

"Okay, Gulliver. You have my attention."

"Have you heard about the detective who was shot on the boardwalk?"

"Sure," Joey said. "It was all over the news. What about him?"

"The detective was named Sam Patrick. He was my friend."

Vespucci's smile went away. "Sorry for your loss. You may not believe this, but I like cops. Flip side of the same coin. Most guys I grew up with became cops. You know what I mean?"

Gullie nodded that he did.

"But that had nothing to do with me, little man. Bad for business to kill cops."

"I know that," Dowd said. "But I don't think it was an accident. I think he was executed. I have to speak to the cop who shot him. The thing is, the cops have him stashed somewhere. I need to know where."

Joey wrinkled his brow. Sipped his scotch. "That's a tough one."

"I'll understand if you can't do it."

"I didn't say that," Joey barked in anger. Then caught himself. "I can do it. But why should I?"

"Because you said you would."

Joey's smile came back. "You got a set on you, little man. I like that. How you come in here like you're the man with the power."

Gullie laughed. "I'm not?"

They both laughed. They finished their drinks.

"Give me a day," Joey said. "I'll get in touch with you."

Gulliver got out of his chair. Shook Joey's hand. "Thanks. I owe you one."

"I'll hold you to that, little man. Don't think I won't. I like you. But business is business."

"I got it, Joey. Business is business."

Vespucci walked Dowd to the study door and said, "You ever hear from Nina?"

Gullie's heart sank. Nina Morton had been the love of Gulliver's life. She had wormed her way back into his heart and life a few years back. She'd begged Dowd to help find her missing daughter. During the search he found out that Joey and Nina had been in business together. That's how Joey and Gullie met. In the end, Nina broke Gulliver's heart a second time. But this time she had paid a bigger price than he had. A much bigger price.

"No, Joey. I haven't heard from her in over a year."

"But you found her girl, right? Man, what a mess that was."

"I found her daughter. Beautiful girl. Smart. A great artist. But she doesn't speak to Nina anymore. She's cut Nina out of her life."

"Too bad for Nina. It would kill me if my girls did that to me," Joey said. He looked behind him at the pictures of his daughters and grandchildren on his mantel. "It would kill me dead."

Gullie shrugged. "She got what she wanted. Then got what she deserved. Sometimes those are the same things. Sometimes not. It blew up in her face."

"Gotta watch out what you wish for, huh? Don't always work out like you think. Oh, well. Take care, little man. We'll talk."

Gulliver left. Joey shut the study door behind him. It was hard for Gullie not to like Vespucci. That bothered him. Gullie wondered why it was that everything Joey said sounded like a warning. Maybe it was.

TEN

Their next stop was back in Brooklyn. Due to his injuries and the death of Sam, Gulliver had put off going to speak to the cops. He had to talk to them about getting run off the road. He knew he couldn't put it off for too long. And he knew something else. That the cops just wanted an explanation. Almost any story would do. The stuff about cops always wanting to find the truth or get to the bottom of things was for TV and the movies. What the cops wanted was to close cases. Period. End of story.

The detective handling Gulliver's case was a young guy named Andy Cohen. Cohen didn't quite choke on his tongue at the sight of Gullie. But he was pretty surprised by the small man who walked into the squad room and introduced himself. He was even more surprised when Gulliver explained that he was a licensed PI. That his sister had been a cop killed on the job. Cohen didn't know what hit him. But if Gullie thought Cohen was so off-balance he would swallow any story he was fed, Gullie was wrong. Just his luck to get some eager young hotshot who still thought the truth was important.

First Cohen had Gulliver review the statement he had given to the highway-patrol cop on the night the van was rammed.

"So, Mr. Dowd, is your statement correct?" asked Cohen.

"It is."

"Why do you think another van ran you off the Belt Parkway?"

"Road rage, maybe. I don't know. I guess you'd have to ask the guy who tried to run me off the road."

"Did you happen to see what he looked like?"

"No, Detective, I was too busy trying to save my life at the time."

Cohen said, "Well, we found his van." He tossed some photos in front of Gullie. "It was stolen. That's it there, on fire. We found it next to what used to be the Fountain Avenue garbage dump."

Gulliver shrugged his shoulders. "Hope the guy the van was taken from has good insurance."

"Weird, don't you think?" Cohen said.

"What?"

"That someone in a stolen van should try to run you off the road. Most car thieves I know try to keep out of trouble."

The detective shook his head. "But this guy seemed to go out of his way to call attention to himself. He comes after you again and again. Bang. Bang. Bang. Until he sends your van skidding off the road."

"Maybe he had a bad temper," Gulliver said. "Road rage doesn't always make sense."

"So this guy steals a van. He rams you with it. Not once. Three times. Then he pulls off the road a few miles east of you and lights the stolen van on fire. Doesn't work for me. What did he do, walk home?"

"Like I said, Detective Cohen, you'll have to ask him."

"You know what I think, Mr. Dowd?"

"No, but I'm sure you're going to tell me."

"I don't think this is a case of road rage at all," Cohen said. "For one thing, the roads were almost empty that night. It was snowing. In your statement you didn't say you cut anyone off or made a risky driving move. In fact, you say you stayed in the right lane."

"I had a concussion when I talked to the cop that night, Detective Cohen. I wasn't exactly in the best shape to remember what I might have done. Maybe I did cut someone off. I don't know."

"Not how I see it, Mr. Dowd. I think the guy who stole that van had only one thing in mind. To come after you. The question is, why? But there's another question. A more interesting one."

"What's that, Detective Cohen?"

"Why are you lying to me about this?"

"Am I lying to you?" Gullie asked. "What do I have to gain by lying to you?"

"Another interesting question. Only you can answer that."

Gulliver hopped down from the chair. "I'm going now, Detective Cohen. It was nice meeting you. If you come up with anything, please let me know."

Cohen shook Gullie's hand.

"I know there's more to this, Mr. Dowd. You know you never told us where you were coming from when your van got hit. Or where you were going."

"You're right," Gullie said, "I didn't."

He didn't feel good about lying to the detective. But he could not risk letting anyone inside the NYPD know he had meant to meet Sam on the night he was killed. Gullie wasn't a trusting person to begin with. And now was not the time to change his ways.

ELEVEN

Mia had called to let him know she was on her way home. Gulliver was waiting. He was making them breakfast. Eggs on the counter. Bread slices in the toaster. Coffee brewing.

Night shifts were tough. Even if you were used to them they were hard. There was just something about working while most of the city was asleep that added a layer of stress to it. Much of Gulliver's work was at night. That was when he found most runaways. When he found most missing kids on the street. Hanging out. Getting high.

Selling drugs. Selling themselves. He had found few runaways when the sun was up. And he knew that Mia had to deal with emergencies all night long. People and their pets. It was a toss-up whether people got more crazed about their kids or their animals. Mia said it was pets. Hands down. You weren't even supposed to call them pets anymore. Now they were animal friends.

Night shift or not, Gulliver liked cooking for Mia. Being there for her. He had been alone for so much of his life that just eating with Mia felt like a gift. When he heard her drop her keys outside the door, Gullie knew something was wrong. That was their signal. She would now pick up the keys. Count to ten. Open the door. Gullie had told Mia to drop her keys if she felt there was danger in the hall. If something was wrong. After Mia had been abducted by her former boss, Gulliver had taught her some tricks. He had showed her how to defend herself. He had taught her to shoot. He had put her on his payroll so he could get her a gun permit. She didn't have one yet. So Gulliver moved quickly now. He quietly went to get his 9mm SIG Sauer. He tucked himself behind the sofa. He would have a clear shot at anyone coming through the door in front of or behind Mia.

Gullie counted to himself. *Seven. Eight. Nine. Ten.* He raised his SIG. The door pushed open. When it did, Mia stepped in. She ran into the kitchen. *Good girl*, Gullie thought. *Just like I taught you.*

And right behind her, a shadow filled up the empty doorway. An arm reached into the apartment. The hand at the end of it knocked on the door.

A familiar voice called out, "Yo, Bug."

It was Joey Vespucci's man, Tony.

"Come in, Tony," Dowd said, stepping out from behind the couch. "Come on out, Mia. It's okay. I know this guy. He's all right."

Tony stepped into the living room as Mia came out of the kitchen.

Gullie pointed to Tony. "Mia, meet Tony. Tony, meet Mia."

They nodded to each other.

"You all want some coffee?" Dowd asked.

"I do," Mia said.

Tony shook his head. "Nah, I'm good. You think we could talk a minute, Dowd?"

"Sure, Tony. Follow me. Mia, I'll be out to have breakfast with you in a few minutes. Do me a favor. Pour me some coffee."

Gullie led Tony into the spare bedroom. He closed the door behind them.

"You done good for yourself, Bug. She's a babe."

"Thanks. I'll tell her you think so. What's up?"

"The cops ain't got that guy stashed like you think," Tony said. "He's got himself hid in a cabin up in Cobleskill. You know it?"

"Between Albany and Cooperstown."

"That's it. He and some other cops own a hunting cabin up there. Here's the address."

Tony handed Gulliver a slip of paper.

"The boss says to watch your shrunken little ass. He says he don't got a good feelin' about this. Me, I couldn't care less if your freakin' head gets blown off. But that wouldn't make the boss happy. So watch out. The boss ain't lasted this long by being wrong a lot."

"You sure you don't want coffee or something to eat?"

Tony looked at Dowd. Confused. "I just said I pretty much hope you get killed and you wanna feed me."

Gullie laughed. "Mia is teaching me to be polite. Besides, I didn't say I wouldn't poison your eggs."

"You're funny, Bug. Remember what the boss says."

When Tony had gone, Gulliver made some scrambled eggs and toast. As he cooked, he told Mia how proud he was of her.

"You handled yourself just right," he said.

"I saw him in the elevator, and then he got out right behind me," she said. "I was scared, Gullie. I'm still shaking. He's a scary-looking man."

"Would it make you feel better if I told you I once smacked him around?"

She made a nervous laugh. "Why?"

Gulliver came around the table and held Mia tightly. "It's okay," he whispered. "It's okay."

She was crying. "I don't think I could go through what I went through with Dr. Prentice again."

Dr. Prentice was Mia's old boss. He had been smuggling rare animals into the country for huge sums of cash. When Mia found some of the cash hidden in the office, Prentice and his henchman had kidnapped her. She had been beaten. They had used her as bait to get to Dowd. Mia was going to a shrink to help her get over things. But it was slow going. She would be just fine for a month or two. Then she would have a week of nightmares. She would wake up screaming. Or Gullie would find her hiding in a closet.

"I can't take that again, Gullie," she said. "Please, I—"

"Shhh. Shhh." He stroked her hair. "I won't let anything like that happen to you again. You'll have your carry permit soon. And your self-defense lessons are going well, right?"

She nodded.

"Come on, you." Gullie took her by the hand. "You need some sleep."

When he was sure Mia was asleep, he called Detective Ralph Rigo.

TWELVE

Rigo drove the two and a half hours up to Cobleskill from Brooklyn. They didn't talk much. Just admired the scenic views. Snow on the Catskill Mountains. The trees. The Hudson River. If you lived in New York City, it was easy to forget the rest of the state was even there. Yet just north of the city were beautiful mountain ranges. Waterfalls. Rivers. Lakes. Whole areas of pristine forest. Gullie had grown up on Long Island. But it had become almost as crowded as the city. A maze of strip malls and traffic jams. Houses built right on top of each other. He liked the drive to Cobleskill.

As they got near the town, Rigo said, "So how did you find this address?"

"Vespucci came through for me. I knew he would. He owed me this favor."

"How did you guys become friends again?"

"I didn't say he was my friend."

"Yeah, sure. Whatever."

That was the last thing they said before they got to within a half mile of the cabin.

"GPS says to make a right down this road here, Dowd. What's our move?"

"We approach in a car, Stevens is going to run," Gullie said. "Let's park the car and go down there on foot. I'll walk a direct path. You circle around back. Through the woods."

Rigo didn't like it. "You think he's just gonna let you walk right in there through the front door?"

"You let me worry about that. People don't know what to make of me. That gets them off their game. I know how to use that. I've been using it all my life."

"And here I was thinking it was your charm and imposing figure," Rigo said.

They both had a laugh at that. Rigo parked the car. They got out. Gulliver nodded to Rigo to go ahead. The fat detective circled around and into the woods as they had planned. Dowd gave him a head start. It would take Rigo longer to get to the cabin. Tony's warning rang in Dowd's ears. *The boss says to watch your shrunken little ass.* Tony was right. Joey Vespucci hadn't lasted this long without knowing a bad thing when he saw it. It was too late to go back now. And Gullie had to find out what had really happened to Sam Patrick. He took a deep breath and started out for the cabin.

As he walked along the rutted dirt road, he thought about Sam. About Keisha.

About himself. A million questions popped into his head all at once. Was he doing this to find the truth about Sam? Or was he doing this to find out about Keisha? Had Gullie's best chance to find out about Keisha's murder died with Sam? Had Sam's death been a mistake? Did Gullie's being run off the road really have anything to do with Sam's death? Or did he want to believe it so much that he was ignoring the facts? One thing about Gulliver. He did not turn away from the truth. No matter what. No matter how hard. No matter how cruel. No matter how much it hurt. And to find the truth, he had to be true with himself. Once he spoke to Stevens, he would know.

The skies were angry. Dark and gray. The clouds looked heavy with water. A freezing wind blew. It felt like a thousand needles hitting his cheeks. The air smelled like snow was coming. It was quiet. Too quiet. There was still some old snow on the ground. It crunched beneath Gullie's shoes. It seemed to be the only sound in the world. Smoke rose from the chimney of the cabin. Something didn't feel right. Gullie could not risk drawing his SIG. He might not look very scary, but a gun looks like a threat no matter who is carrying it. Even if it's a little shrimpy guy with a handsome face. Instead, Gullie slipped his knife up his sleeve. Then, when he was about halfway down the road—*bang!*

A shot rang out. It broke the silence. It echoed loudly in the woods for what felt like forever to Gullie. A door slammed.

"Dowd! Dowd! Hurry up! Get the fuck over here!" It was Rigo.

Gulliver hated to run. One of his legs was shorter than the other. He could hide his slight limp when he walked. Not when he ran. When he ran, his limp became a hobble. The faster he ran, the worse the hobble got. If he ran too fast, he would topple over. So he ran as fast as he dared.

The front door of the cabin was locked. Gulliver went around back. Here, the door was standing open. He stepped inside. Slowly, carefully, he walked ahead.

"Rigo. Where are you, Rigo?"

"Up here, Dowd. In the second bedroom to the right of the stairs. It's safe."

But even before he got to the bedroom, he knew it was bad. Gullie could smell the spent gunpowder. Smell the gunsmoke. Smell the copper-iron mist of blood in the air. He could almost taste it.

All those odors were much stronger inside the bedroom. Rigo was there. His Smith & Wesson in his hand. His gun hand down at his side. The body of a man lay on the bed. A .357 Magnum Colt next to the body's right hand. Blood. Hair. Bits of bone and brain were sprayed against one wall.

"He ate his gun," Rigo said. "I heard the shot just as I got to the back door. By the time I got up here..." Rigo shrugged his shoulders. "Too late."

"Stevens?"

"Yeah, it's him."

Gulliver said, "Someone is tying up loose ends. Now I know Sam was murdered."

"But there's a suicide note," Rigo said. "Over there on the night table. Says he felt too guilty over killing Sam. He couldn't take it no more. Look for yourself."

Suddenly, Joey Vespucci's warning came back into Dowd's head. Things weren't right. Rigo was sweating as if he had run all the way to the house. He was shaking too. There were speckles of blood on his hands and coat. Gullie looked at the blood on the wall. It was too high up. If Stevens had shot himself, he was standing when he did it. How many people shoot themselves standing up? Gullie had trouble believing Stevens would have. And how had Rigo gotten into the house? It didn't make sense that Stevens would leave the back door open when he was hiding out. Then Gullie saw a picture on the wall. It was of a group of men standing around the body of a buck deer. They all had their hands on the antlers. One of the men was Stevens. One of them was Sam Patrick. Another was Rigo.

Shit! It was a trap. Gulliver had been set up. Rigo had played the part of the angry partner to get close to Gulliver. To get Gullie alone. And if Gulliver got too nosy or too close to the truth, Rigo would get rid of him. It all made sense now. Gulliver was just another loose end to tie up. Rigo had keys to the place. He had let himself in. He had put the computer-printed suicide note on the nightstand. He'd killed Stevens with a drop piece. Now Rigo would kill Gulliver. Dump his body out in the woods. Or throw it into the quarry lake they had passed on the way up to the cabin. Joey Vespucci was right not to like this. It had probably been too easy for him to find out where Stevens was hiding. Now Gullie was angry at himself for not drawing his SIG. If Rigo tried something here in the bedroom, he would be a dead man.

But Rigo said, "C'mon, let's go outside. We'll call it in." He hadn't figured out that Gulliver knew the truth.

Gullie liked the idea of going outside. Outside, he had a fighting chance. Room to move. Places to hide. But he didn't like that Rigo kept his Smith & Wesson in his hand. If he walked ahead of Rigo, the fat man might just shoot him in the back.

"He killed himself, Rigo," Gulliver said, adding a laugh. "You can holster your gun now. Stevens can't shoot you by accident. He just did the last shooting he's ever going to do."

Rigo laughed a nervous laugh. "Yeah, yeah, you're right, Dowd." He holstered his Smith & Wesson.

"I've got to get out of here. I'm feeling kind of sick," Gulliver lied. But it gave him an excuse to run out of the cabin as fast as he could. To get a head start on Rigo.

Gulliver was halfway down the stairs by the time Rigo caught on. The fat man came charging after him. Gulliver was almost at the back door when he heard the shot. *Bang!* Wood splintered to the left of his head. *Bang! Bang! Bang!* The shots came in a quick burst. One after the other. But Rigo was a bad shot when he was moving. It was one thing to stick a gun in a man's mouth and pull the trigger. Like he had done to Stevens. It was much harder to hit a moving target while he was moving too. And when that moving target was Gulliver's size... Sometimes being small was a good thing. Gulliver could have gotten to his SIG. The problem was, he didn't want to kill Rigo. How would he explain killing an NYPD detective? How would he explain Stevens's body?

How would he explain any of it? He also wanted to talk to Rigo. Rigo was part of something much bigger. Something connected to Sam's murder. To Keisha's murder. First, he had to buy himself time.

Once out of the cabin, Gulliver ducked into the woods. Rigo knew the area. That's how he had gotten to the cabin so fast. But Gullie didn't have a lot of options. He couldn't risk staying out in the open. The woods would give him places to hide. Another good thing about the woods was that it had a built-in alarm system. Woods are covered in fallen branches. Twigs. Dried leaves. Old snow. And Rigo was a fat man. Gulliver would be able to hear if Rigo was getting close. He could wait Rigo out. Wait until it got dark. Then he could sneak out of the woods

THIRTEEN

Within a few minutes Gulliver had found a good hiding spot. It was a place where many trees had fallen over one another. A gap in between them that only a kid or someone like Gullie could squeeze into. Spaces between the fallen trees gave him a full view of the woods. Rigo would not be able to get close without Gullie seeing or hearing him. When he caught his breath, he texted Ahmed to get Mia. To take her to a safe location. Until this was over, he had to keep Mia out of it. Until that morning, Gulliver had not understood just how fragile Mia was. Nothing was worth risking her. Ahmed texted back that he would take care of it.

It was quiet in the woods. As if not even the birds felt like singing. Then snow began to fall. Gulliver sat back. Relaxed. Killing time until Ahmed texted that Mia was safe. Until night began to set in many hours from now. Until he could work his way out of the woods and into town.

But life hardly ever works the way you plan it. A shot echoed through the forest. The log above Gulliver's head rocked. Splintered. Pieces of wood flew into the air.

Uh-oh, Gullie thought. *Rigo went back and got a hunting rifle*. Rigo may have been fat, but he was a good hunter. Gulliver was in big trouble now. He didn't hunt. He didn't like being hunted. He might have no choice but to shoot back at Rigo. It might not matter. His SIG was built for short-range shooting. Good for only a few hundred feet at best. Rigo's hunting rifle was built to hit small targets from hundreds of yards away. If Gulliver stood up now, he was dead for sure. If he ran, he was dead. If he waited, he might end up dead. But if he waited, Rigo might well get within range of Gulliver's SIG.

Gulliver got out his pistol. Undid the safety. Racked the slide to put a cartridge in the chamber. He forced himself to relax. He used breathing tricks he'd learned from his jujitsu and karate teachers. It was a while before he heard Rigo's footsteps snapping twigs. For such a heavy man, Rigo made much less noise than Gullie had thought he would. Just because Gulliver got judged by how he looked didn't mean he didn't do the same thing. He had misjudged Rigo. Fat or not, Rigo had a big advantage over Gullie. He listened as Rigo got closer. Closer. Closer. Then, when Gulliver thought he would have a clear shot, he poked his head up.

Rested his weapon on the top log. Aimed. But Rigo was not there.

"Over here, you stupid little prick. Put your piece on the tree and turn around. Slow. Real slow."

Gulliver did as he was told. Put the SIG down. Turned around. Rigo didn't see the knife Gulliver had slid down into his palm from the sleeve of his coat. Rigo was standing about twenty feet behind him.

"I know these woods like the back of my hand," Rigo said. "You wasn't gonna get away from me, you shrimpy bastard."

"You killed Stevens."

"Yeah. But by the time I get done, it'll look like you done it." Rigo was proud of himself.

"I don't think so. You screwed up, Rigo. You shot him while he was still standing. If he was sitting on the bed, maybe."

"How can you know that?" Rigo was mad. So mad he wasn't keeping his mind on the rifle in his hands. The tip of the rifle was now no longer aimed right at Gulliver.

"The blood spatter on the wall behind him was way high up on the wall. I would have to stand on a ladder to shoot him like that. And I'm not sure he would've stood still long enough for that. Plus, that Colt is a beast. You think the cops will believe Stevens just stood there while I climbed up the ladder and hoisted the Colt up?"

Rigo raised the rifle. "It don't matter nohow. You're gonna die. You little piece of shit."

"Think for a minute, you moron," Gulliver shouted. "You're here to tie up loose ends. But you're a loose end. After you killed Stevens. After you've killed me. They're going to kill you. Why not tell me what's going on here? I can get you clear of it."

The look on Rigo's face said it all. He realized what Gullie had said was true. At least, the first part. He was as good as dead himself. But he was in too deep to get out of it.

"Too late in the game, Dowd. I'll kill you and split. By the time anyone cares, this will all be over."

"It won't be over until you're dead, Rigo."

Rigo hesitated just long enough for Gulliver to throw his knife. It was a waste. Before the knife had traveled a foot, another shot echoed through the trees. Rigo's body swayed sideways. The knife missed. It stuck in a tree next to Rigo's right shoulder. Rigo's face went blank. Blood poured out of his mouth. He fell face first. His head smacked into the trunk of a fallen tree. It made a sickening sound. But Rigo was too dead to care. The snow-covered ground around Rigo's body turned red. Gullie was right. Rigo was a loose end that needed tying. One bullet had just done that.

But while the bullet had tied up someone else's loose ends, it created new ones for

Gullie. And new questions. Stevens and Rigo were dead. Sam was dead. Who was behind their deaths? Why? Why had someone killed Rigo but not him? Those were questions for later. The shooter might change his mind and take Gullie out.

Gulliver dug his knife out of the tree. He ran as fast as he dared through the woods. He didn't hear anyone behind him. But he could not afford to be too sure. By dusk he had found a state highway. A trucker hauling spare auto parts down to New York City gave him a lift. Gullie laughed to himself. He thought of himself as being made out of spare parts. Parts that didn't match. That didn't matter. At least he was alive. He had left two dead men behind him. He had no wish to join them.

FOURTEEN

It was nearly 8:00 PM when Gulliver got back to the apartment. He tried calling Mia's cell many times. It always went straight to voice mail. He left messages. She never called back. He wondered if she was really mad at him. Or if Ahmed had told her to keep her phone turned off so she couldn't be tracked. Gulliver hoped it was that and not that she was angry with him. But even if she was mad, it didn't matter. He had promised her he wouldn't let anything happen to her. He already felt guilty about what had happened to her last year. It was his case that had gotten Mia kidnapped and almost murdered. And all because he had brought a dog into her vet clinic. He wasn't going to let that happen again. Even if it meant ruining their love. Even if it meant sacrificing himself. Just like how he never backed down from the truth. He always tried to keep his promises. With this promise, trying wasn't good enough. Gulliver still didn't know what this was all about. But one thing was clear as crystal. The people who had murdered Sam Patrick meant business. They had killed Officer Stevens and Detective Rigo just to cover their tracks. And someone had tried to run Dowd off the road. He could not let Mia anywhere near this case.

Ahmed rapped a coded knock on Gulliver's apartment door. Gullie unlocked the door and stepped back. He pointed his SIG at the door. Ahmed stepped inside. He latched the locks behind him. Gullie put down his 9mm.

"Is Mia safe?" he asked.

"Yeah, man, she's safe."

"Where is she?" Gulliver asked.

Ahmed shook his head. "Sorry, little man. It's safer for her if you don't know. They can't get to her, it's harder for them to get to you."

Gullie didn't like it. But he knew Ahmed was right. It was another layer of protection for Mia.

"If it makes you feel better," Ahmed said, "I don't even know where she's at. I put her in the hands of people I trust. When it's safe, they'll bring her to us."

He handed Gulliver a cell phone. He didn't speak. Instead, he handed a note to Gulliver. It said:

Can't be sure someone ain't listening.

Have your apartment checked for bugs.

This is a prepaid cell you can use to call Mia.

The number was written down as well. Gulliver put the cell in his pocket. He memorized the number. He tore the note into tiny pieces. Threw the pieces in the sink. Washed them down the drain.

"Come on, let's take a ride," Gulliver said. "I'm hungry."

But they didn't take a ride. They just stepped out into the hall to talk. Gulliver told Ahmed all about what had happened with Detective Rigo.

"That's some scary shit, little man."

"Tell me about it. You see why I've got to protect Mia."

Ahmed nodded. "These guys mean to clean house. To tie up loose ends. You know what it's about?"

"No. But some stuff is clear. Sam Patrick, Detective Rigo, and Officer Stevens all knew each other. They all shared a secret. It's a secret that involves at least one other person. And that other person will do anything not to have the secret come out. He's willing to murder his friends.

He's willing to murder me. But now I finally have an idea why Keisha was murdered."

Ahmed's eyes got big. "She knew the secret too."

"Bingo. She knew the secret. And they were afraid she would tell. It must have been about something going on in the Seven-Five precinct. Maybe she overheard guys talking. Who knows?"

"But why start killing all these dudes now?" Ahmed asked. "It's been seven, eight years since Keisha been dead. It don't make no sense."

"Maybe it does. What if one of the people who knew the secret decided to tell me?"

"Sam!"

"That's right, Ahmed. That's why Sam wanted to meet with me the night he was murdered on the boardwalk. He was going to tell me why Keisha had been killed. These other guys must have been keeping an eye on Sam. When they figured out he was going to give them up—"

"They had to get rid of him. Man, Dowd, this is crazy."

"Once Sam Patrick was killed, the dominos started falling. Stevens killed Sam. Rigo killed Stevens. He was going to kill me."

Ahmed said, "I guess they figured if Sam could decide to tell, they couldn't trust each other no more."

"That's how secrets fall apart. Once the wall cracks a little, the whole thing crumbles."

"You got any idea what the secret is?" Ahmed asked.

"No. Could be drugs. Could be prostitution. Could be something big or small. Right now it doesn't matter what it is. Only two things matter for now."

"What's that, little man?"

"One, keeping Mia safe. And two, finding out why Sam wanted to tell me now. He could have told me anytime in the last year. So why now? I think if we find that out, we'll have the rest of our answers."

Ahmed nodded. It all made sense. Twisted. Deadly. Bloody sense.

FIFTEEN

Gulliver listened to the rings. His heart beat hard. Very hard. He wanted Mia to pick up more than he had ever wanted anything. In that moment he realized again how scary love could be. There had been many such moments since Mia had said the words, *I love you, Gulliver Dowd. I love you more than I thought it was possible to love anyone.* It had felt as if she had stolen the words from his mouth. He felt exactly the same way. And their love was a grown-up love. It made the love he had once had for Nina Morton seem almost silly.

With Nina it was more a dream of what love was supposed to be than real love. It was a teenager's dream of love. Gullie had to admit that the teenage love for Nina had lasted many years. Too many years. But it could not touch the deep feelings he had for Mia. He trusted Mia. He trusted Mia's love.

"Hello." Her voice was sleepy.

"Hi, you," Gullie said. Afraid.

"When I get out of here, I'm going to make love to you for a week. Then I'm going to kill you, Gulliver Dowd."

He smiled. His heart beat even faster." I love you too, Mia."

"I'm mad at you, Gullie. Why—"

"I just had to make sure you were safe. I'm sure Ahmed told you. Things are dangerous for me. For anyone around me. I can't let anything happen to you because of me. Not after last year."

"But—"

"No buts, hon. Call me selfish. But I need you. I love you. I want you forever. What would I do without you, Mia?"

"You'd survive."

"I wouldn't want to without you." he said.

"Come on, Gullie. People always say that."

"But I mean it. Be as mad at me as you want. But nothing can happen to you on my watch."

"Okay."

"Where are you?" he asked.

"I don't know. I was blindfolded and driven somewhere for hours. Then I got on a plane. I could be anywhere. It's warm here. I can tell you that."

Gulliver knew this part was probably a lie she had been told to tell him. The truth was, Mia was probably still in the New York metro area. But anyone listening to their call wouldn't know that.

"Enjoy the sun. You are so pretty with a tan," he said.

"And I'm not pretty without one?" she joked.

"I love you, Mia."

"I love you more."

"Not possible," he said. "Not possible. Bye."

He held the phone in his hand for a long time. It was as if he was holding Mia.

SIXTEEN

Gulliver was sitting at the table missing Mia when his phone rang. It was Sam Patrick's ex-wife, Mary. She sounded like she had been crying.

"Gullie," she said. "Gullie, I don't know what to do."

"What's wrong, Mary?"

"It's Sam's will."

"What about it?" Gulliver asked.

"His lawyer hasn't called me about it yet. I'm the executor. I have a copy of it. But Sam has been dead for days and I haven't heard a word from the lawyer."

"That's weird. Unless the lawyer lives under a rock or he's on vacation, he should have called. Have you called him?"

"So many times I've lost count. His phone message says nothing about him being away. The funeral is tomorrow and—"

"It's okay, Mary. I'll pay a visit to his office and check it out."

"Oh, Gullie, that would be great."

"Glad to do it. Just give me his address, and I'll handle it."

Gulliver's first call after he'd gotten off the phone with Mary was to his childhood friend Steven Mandel. Gullie called Steve Rabbi. Steven wasn't really a rabbi. He was a hotshot lawyer. But Gulliver had always called him Rabbi. Why? Gullie couldn't remember why. He had started calling Steve that when they were kids. He thought it might be because Steve was always wise beyond his years. He was always big-hearted, a caring guy. Whatever the reason, the nickname had stuck. Now even Mia called him Rabbi.

"Hey, Gullie, what's up?" Rabbi asked.

"You know a lawyer named Arnold J. Gold?"

"Sure, I know Arnie. He used to have a big criminal practice. Big cases. Lots of mob work. Then he gave it up a few years back. Went into estate planning. Stuff like that. Last I heard, he was running a one-man office out in Forest Hills. Why do you ask?"

Gullie didn't want to get Rabbi involved in this mess. So he told a small lie to his pal. "A friend of a friend wants to use him for a will. He asked me if there was anything shady about this Gold guy. So I'm asking you," Gullie said.

"Nothing shady that I know of. Arnie did quit the criminal practice kind of out of the blue. But I never heard whispers or anything. Sometimes people just can't deal with the pressure anymore. That it?"

"For now, yeah."

"How's the beautiful Mia doing?" Rabbi asked.

"Safe and sound."

"You guys up for a double date this weekend? I met somebody."

Rabbi was always meeting somebody. Dark. Tall. Lean. He had movie-star looks. Women loved him. And he loved them right back.

"Maybe not this weekend, Rabbi. Can we take a rain check?"

"You know it," Rabbi said. "But I can't promise my date will be the same woman as would have come this weekend."

"Your idea of settling down is a second date."

"What can I tell you, Gullie? Not all of us are lucky enough to have a Mia in our lives."

"Amen to that. Talk to you soon."

* * *

Arnold J. Gold's office address was on a small side street off Yellowstone Boulevard. It was in a red brick house that was attached to the houses on its left and right. Gold rented his office space from a family that lived on the top floor. His office was in the downstairs apartment. There was a sign out front on a wrought-iron pole:

Arnold J. Gold

Attorney-at-Law

There was a black Mercedes Benz 300 parked on the street near the driveway. It had once been a nice car. Now it was old. Its paint faded. Its body dinged up. The license plate was a vanity plate—*GO 4 GOLD*. Gullie figured it had to be the lawyer's car. He had Ahmed park in front of the Mercedes. When they got out of Ahmed's Escalade, they knew something was wrong.

"Look at the windshield, little man."

"Tickets for illegal parking. You're supposed to switch sides of the street every day but Wednesday."

"Do the math," Ahmed said.

"He hasn't moved his car since the day Sam was killed."

"True, that. Let's be real careful."

They walked slowly to the entrance of Gold's office. The door was closed. Not locked. The knob turned in Gulliver's hand. Even before they got the door all the way open, they smelled it. Death was in the air. It was thick with it. Gulliver and Ahmed covered their mouths and noses. Gullie turned to Ahmed.

"Give me five minutes in here. Then use one of those prepaid cell phones I gave you. Call it in. Don't use your name."

Ahmed nodded. Went back to his Caddy to wait. He was happy to get out of the stink.

Gulliver put on the latex gloves he always carried. He walked into the office. He found the lawyer's body behind his desk. From the ugly marks on Gold's neck, it looked like he had been strangled. The dead man's eyes were open. They had turned a milky white in color. Gulliver had seen many dead bodies. Some close up. He didn't like it. He would never get used to it.

He moved carefully around the body. He searched the file drawers. Just as he knew it would be, Sam Patrick's file was gone. The computer monitor and keyboard were still on the lawyer's desk. The computer tower was missing. But Gold's killer had made at least one mistake. He had left the lawyer's old-fashioned appointment book on the desk. Using a pencil, Gullie turned the pages to the day Sam was killed. Scribbled in red was the entry *Emergency meeting Sam P. 1 PM. Package for GD.*

GD had to stand for Gulliver Dowd. But what was the package Sam had meant to give him? Now Gullie was sure there was a secret. A secret Sam was going to reveal to Gulliver the night he was killed. The secret was so important that now a fourth person had been killed to protect it. But what was the secret? Was the secret in the package? Was the secret the package itself? And why was Sam finally going to tell Gulliver about it? Gullie didn't have time to think about that now. He had to get out of the office. On the way out, he rubbed his fingerprints off the front doorknob.

It was good to smell fresh air again. But the image of Gold's milky eyes would haunt Gulliver for days to come.

They sped away from Gold's office. Down Yellowstone Boulevard and past the 112th Precinct. They spotted two squad cars racing in the other direction.

"Well," Gullie said, "it won't take them long to get there."

"Was he murdered or was it, like, a heart attack or something?" Ahmed asked.

"Strangled."

"Find anything?"

Gullie shook his head in disgust. "Nothing I can use as evidence. Nothing that will prove anything to anybody. Just that I know the lawyer was preparing a package for me. Maybe Sam was going to give it to me. Maybe the lawyer. But I don't have it. And I still don't know what the secret is."

"But you got something else bugging you, little man. I can tell."

"One question keeps going around and around in my head. It's like at night when a mosquito keeps buzzing by your ear. You swat at it, but it won't go away. Keeps coming back every few seconds."

"What's the question? Maybe I can help," Ahmed offered.

"Maybe. Maybe not. It's that same old question. Why now? Why did this all happen now? Why did Sam pick that day to tell me? I still feel like if I can just find out why he picked that day...I don't know. Maybe if I know why, I can figure out what the secret is."

Ahmed nodded. "Maybe it's something stupid like in the movies."

"What do you mean?"

"Like when a guy says, 'If you kill me, my lawyer will deliver proof to the cops,'" said Ahmed. "You know, some shit like that."

"Doesn't usually work that way."

"I'm just saying is all."

"Right now it's the best idea we've got. It's the only idea we've got. Too bad life isn't like the movies."

Gulliver dialed Mary to tell her about the dead lawyer.

SEVENTEEN

The interior of the church was a sea of blue uniforms. Cop funerals are always a big deal in New York City. They are an even bigger deal when the cop is killed in the line of duty. There were cops from all over the northeast. From all over the country. Some from Canada too. Gulliver didn't like that Mia wasn't there with him. That he would have to lie about why. But he had to protect her. He felt like things were getting more dangerous. Not safer. He made his way through the crowd to Mary. He nodded for her to come have a chat with him for a second. She stood right up.

"You should be able to clear the will up now that they found the lawyer's body," Gullie said.

"Do you really think his murder is connected to—"

Gullie shushed her. "Don't say it. But yes. It's one hundred percent connected. And it's connected to me somehow. I don't know how yet."

"You'll find out. I know you will. Sam once told me he thought you were a better detective than all the guys he worked with."

"Yeah, but they're taller. I would trade for that in a second."

That made Mary smile. But Gulliver was serious. He *would* have traded. But he wasn't going to rob Mary of that smile. She had been robbed of too much already.

"You were married when Sam worked in the Seven-Five, right?" Gulliver asked.

"When we bought our house. Bought our boat. Put the down payment on our place in Florida. We were strong then. Really in love. Then things changed."

Mary broke down as she looked over at Sam's coffin. Gullie comforted her. It wasn't the time to ask her more questions. He waded in among the cops. Listening for any rumors floating around. Listening to hear if the upstate cops had found the bodies of Stevens and Rigo.

That was another plus of Gulliver's size. People sometimes didn't notice he was there. Even if they did, they often didn't care. People said stuff in front of Gulliver that they would never have said in front of a normal-size man. People tended to think his size meant that he was stupid. Or deaf. Or childlike. He was none of those things.

They hadn't found the bodies yet. Gulliver knew that because he had overheard some guys from the Seven-Six bitching about Rigo. *What an asshole. His partner gets killed and he don't even show up at the funeral.* Gulliver moved on. Then there was quiet in the crowd because the ceremony was about to start. Gullie got a good seat, two rows behind the mayor. Gulliver sat right next to an NYPD big shot from the brass. The guy had lots of shiny metal and stripes and ribbons on his uniform. But Gullie didn't know him. The funeral went the way these things went. There was a lot of praying. A lot of crying. A lot of speeches. Too many speeches. Gulliver wondered how getting shot by accident made Sam a hero.

Then the world changed when the big-brass cop leaned over to the guy next to him. That man was in a dark gray suit. He had a shock of white hair on his head. Gullie knew him. He was in the papers and on TV all the time. His name was Jack O'Connell. He was once a famous detective. Now he was the head of the detectives' union.

The big-shot cop whispered to O'Connell. It was just loud enough for Gullie to hear too. "Sam Patrick, bless his soul, the poor damned bastard."

"How's that?" O'Connell wanted to know.

"Haven't you seen the medical examiner's report?" the big shot asked.

"No. Why should I? I run a union. Wasn't Patrick shot to death by that ass Stevens?"

"True," the big-shot cop said. "But bullet or no bullet, he had no more than a few months to live anyway."

"Explain yourself," O'Connell said.

"Cancer, Jack. Sam Patrick's body was riddled with it. Pancreas. Lungs. Liver. He was a goner. Then that fool Stevens…Ah, maybe he did Sam a favor. Saved him a lot of suffering."

Gulliver could barely breathe. He had his answer. That's why Sam had decided to tell him about Keisha. He was dying. He wanted to get it off his chest. All bets were off. The secret was no longer safe with him. He had nothing to lose. Threats and money lose their power over a dying man. Men with nothing to lose can't be trusted. Somehow, the others had found out about Sam's illness. When they did, they began keeping an eye on him. When Sam went to see Arnie Gold, he sealed his own fate. His lawyer's fate too. And if Gulliver Dowd wasn't such a good driver, he would have been dead as well.

There was someone he had to go see. A doctor.

EIGHTEEN

Tracking down Sam's doctor was easy enough for a PI like Gulliver Dowd. Not because he was a great detective. Nothing like that. It was because Gullie used the same doctor as Sam Patrick. Sam had sent him to Dr. Gupta when Gulliver had a bad sinus infection. His office was only a few hundred yards from the Seven-Six. A lot of the cops there used him.

Rajiv Gupta was a happy-faced man with a big white smile. He had mocha-colored skin. Intense brown eyes. And those eyes lit up at the sight of Gulliver

Dowd walking into his office. The light in them dimmed when they saw Ahmed Foster walk in behind Gullie.

"Mr. Gulliver. How are you, sir?" asked the doctor in his lilting voice. He offered his right hand.

Gulliver shook it.

"Hello, Doc." He did not introduce Ahmed.

Ahmed just stared at the doctor.

"My nurse tells me you are not ill. So what can I do for you and your friend?"

"Ahmed isn't my friend. He kind of watches my back. He's an ex–Navy Seal. He has a nasty habit of breaking things."

"Yes, well…" The doctor was nervous. That was exactly what Gullie wanted.

Gulliver asked, "Did you know that Sam Patrick's funeral was earlier today?"

Gupta shook his head. "Terrible. Terrible about Sam. He was a nice man. It was a pity what happened to him."

"Maybe not," Gulliver said. "I hear he was going to face a lot of pain. A lot of suffering."

Gupta's eyes got wide with fear. "How can you know that?"

"About Sam's cancer? About how it had spread? Let's say I overheard it."

"But he made me promise to tell no one," the doctor said. "He said he wasn't going to tell anyone of his fate."

Gulliver's voice grew cold. "Let's you and me stop worrying about what I know. About how I know it. Let's talk about who else knew. About how they knew it."

Gupta's hands began to shake. He looked at Ahmed. Ahmed looked back without blinking.

"I don't understand," said the doctor.

"Yes, you do, Doc. But we'll get to that in a minute. First I want to know why Sam was coming to a local doctor about cancer."

"Oh, I sent him to the best specialists at Sloan Kettering. But it was all rather hopeless. He had waited too long to come to me with his symptoms. And by the time I sent him to Sloan Kettering…it was much, much too late. After that, Sam asked that I handle his pain medication. He didn't want to go to Sloan Kettering any longer if there was no hope. I am so sorry. I liked Sam very much."

"Then why did you sell him out, Doc?" Gullie asked. "You were updating someone about Sam's health. Weren't you?"

Tears ran down Gupta's brown cheeks. "I had no choice, Mr. Gulliver. They made threats against my family. They showed me video of my children being taken to and coming home from their schools. They threatened the life of my wife. What would you have done in such a case?"

"I'm not here to get you into trouble, Doc. But I want all the truth."

"Whatever you say, Mr. Gulliver. I have felt great guilt over this. I will do whatever you ask."

"Tell me how they approached you," Gullie said.

"One day as I was leaving my office, a man came up to me in the street by my car. He was a scary man. Not so tall as your Mr. Ahmed. But he was thick in the chest and arms. He seemed almost to have no neck. He spoke roughly to me. He said he wanted me to tell him about Sam's illness. That I was to call him after each of Sam's visits. Then he showed me video of my children. Photos of my wife's movements near our home. When I said that I could not do this, he showed me his gun. He stuck it in my belly. He said, *Killing you will be as easy as breathing for me*. He said that he would do terrible things to my wife and children."

"So you gave this man updates?"

Gupta bowed his head in shame. "I did. I did not feel I had a choice."

"Okay, Doc, I can see that. You have to protect the people you love no matter what."

"Still, I feel guilt. I have caused the death of Detective Sam."

"No, Doc. I have a feeling Sam did that to himself. He did something many years ago that began a slow march to his murder."

"What did Detective Sam do?"

"That I can't answer yet," Gulliver said. "Did Sam come to see you on the day he was killed?"

"Yes. He was beginning to get very, very sick. The pain medication was not working so well. His vital signs were getting very weak."

"He was dying?"

"He would not have lasted very much longer, Mr. Gulliver. A month. A week. Days. I cannot say. But he knew it was bad."

"And you told this to the man who wanted updates?"

"Right after Detective Sam left my office," said Gupta.

"Do you have a phone number for this man?"

Gupta did not answer. Instead, he pulled a slip of paper from a drawer. He handed it to Gulliver.

"Thanks, Doc."

Gulliver turned to go.

"Will my family be in danger?" Gupta called after him.

"I don't think so," Gullie said. "And Doc..."

"Yes, Mr. Gulliver?"

"I'll be finding a new doctor to look after me."

Dr. Gupta did not say another word.

Outside, Gulliver dialed the number Gupta had given him. A man picked up after two rings.

"Yeah," the man said. "What is it?"

Gulliver knew the voice. The man had stood in Gulliver's apartment only a few days earlier.

The man on the other end grew impatient. "What is it? Who the fuck is this?"

"It's me, Tony, Gulliver Dowd. Tell your boss to give me a call."

"How the fuck did you get this number, Bug?"

"Just tell your boss I'll be waiting for his call."

Gullie hung up. He went home to wait.

NINETEEN

The parachute jump rose twenty-five stories into the night sky. It was like a big skeleton of steel. Bones with no meat. The top of it always reminded Gulliver Dowd of an umbrella with its fabric torn away. That night most of its upper half was swallowed up by clouds. The ocean was loud. Louder than normal, Gulliver thought. The winds off the water were cold. No one else seemed to be on the boardwalk for miles in either direction. Gulliver was used to feeling alone in the world. He tried to remember if he had ever felt quite this alone before. He knew he was risking his life. But sometimes a man just has to know things. He has to know them no matter what the cost. Dowd heard footsteps on the wooden planks behind him.

"Hello, little man." It was Joey Vespucci.

"Hello, Joey. You alone?"

"Didn't I promise you I would be on the phone?"

"You can't blame me for asking," Gulliver said. "A lot of people have been killed. Some by their friends and partners in this mess."

"I guess that's fair. Yeah, Dowd, I'm alone."

"Why are we here, Joey? Why didn't you just have me killed like all the others?"

"None of the killing was my idea. That's right. Even I have bosses. Everybody's got someone above them. It may not look that way on TV. But believe me, this isn't about me. It's not about you."

Gullie shook his head. "When it involves my murdered sister, when it involves a murdered friend, it involves me."

"Come over by the rail with me. I like looking out at the ocean," Joey said. "Even on a night like this."

They walked over to the guardrail. Joey leaned down. He rested his chin on his folded arms.

"You would be dead a hundred times over by now if I wanted you dead. I stuck my neck out for you so that you're not dead. My bosses wanted you dead. It would've made things easier all around. If you remember, Tony passed a warning on from me. You ever stop to think why you weren't killed up in the woods there in Cobleskill? You know, after the sniper plugged that fat fuck Rigo, he had you in his sights. But he had orders to leave you be. Orders from me."

"I guess this is where I say thanks," Gullie said.

"You're welcome."

"Are you going to tell me what this is all about?"

"I can't do that, Dowd."

"Even though my sister was murdered. Even though many other people have died. You're not going to tell me."

"That's up to you, little man," Joey said. "You've got a big choice to make tonight. The biggest kind of choice a man has to make."

Gullie was confused. "How's that?"

Joey reached into his coat. When Joey did that, Gulliver was tempted to shoot the mob boss. Or stab him. Or disable him with a kick. Instead, Gullie did nothing. Though Joey was a murderer, he had always kept his word to Dowd. When Joey showed Gulliver his hand, he was not holding a gun. Instead, he held a thick brown envelope out in front of him. The envelope was addressed to Gulliver.

"What's that?" Dowd asked.

"This is the envelope Sam Patrick was going to have his lawyer give you when he died. It's got everything in it that you wanna know. Why your sister was killed and all of that. All your questions will be answered," Joey said. "It's yours if you want it."

"Of course I want it, Joey."

"Maybe not, Dowd. Maybe you should listen to me first," Joey said.

"I'm listening."

"If you take the package, you'll have your answers. But you and your pretty girl-friend will be dead by the end of the week. Not many days left in the week. And my bosses say it won't be an easy death for either of you."

"And if I don't take the envelope?" Gullie said.

"You don't take it. You promise to stop nosing around about it. That's that. It's over. Forgotten. We put a match to this envelope.

145

We move on. You. Me. My bosses. You have my word. So that's your choice, little man. You can die knowing about your sister or you can save your girlfriend's life. Not both."

"Do you know why Keisha was killed, Joey?"

"No. And I don't wanna know."

"Do you know who killed her?"

Joey hesitated. "Yeah. I know."

"Can you tell me that much?" Gulliver was almost begging. "Can you please tell me that?"

"Dowd, I know you probably hate my guts right about now. I would hate me too. But I like you. I respect you. Take my advice. Please just leave it alone for your own good. Some things you don't wanna know."

"Who killed her, Joey? Please tell me."

"The guy who killed her is dead, little man. He got what he deserved this week. Leave it there. For your own sake."

"Stevens? Rigo? Which one of those bastards killed my sister?"

"Please, Dowd. Please don't ask. You won't like the answer."

"Stevens? Rigo?" Gulliver repeated. "Which one?"

"Neither. It was your buddy, Sam Patrick. He killed her. See? I told you you wouldn't like the answer."

Gulliver felt like he had been kicked in the stomach. He didn't want to believe Joey. But Gulliver knew Joey was telling the truth.

"I told you not to ask, little man."

"You did."

"So what's it gonna be?" Joey asked.

"You got a match?"

"Better. Here's my lighter. I had it since I was a little punk." Joey Vespucci handed Gulliver his old Zippo.

Gulliver took the lighter. He took the envelope from Joey. He set the envelope on fire.

When it was in flames, when he could not hold it any longer, he threw it onto the sand. They watched it burn. They watched the ashes fly away in the wind like ghosts in black shrouds.

Joey finally spoke. "That was the smart move, Dowd. A man has to enjoy what he has. Your sister is gone. Nothing is gonna change that. You know who did it. Does it matter why anymore?"

"Not if it puts Mia in danger. She's safe. Right?"

Joey held out his right hand to Gulliver. Gulliver didn't want to shake it. But he knew he had to. He shook Joey's hand.

"You have my word," Joey said.

That was good enough for Gulliver.

"Goodbye, Joey."

"Goodbye, little man."

Gulliver turned. Walked away. Silent tears rolled down his cheeks. They were tears of grief. Tears of anger. Tears of joy.

Mostly joy. He would soon have Mia back in his arms. He dialed Ahmed's number. When Ahmed picked up, Gullie said, "Bring her home. Bring Mia home."

ACKNOWLEDGMENTS

I would like to express my deep appreciation to Bob Tyrrell and all the folks at Orca for giving Gulliver his big chance. Also a nod to my agent, David Hale Smith at Inkwell Management.

But mostly I have to thank Rosanne, Kaitlin and Dylan. Without them, none of this would mean a thing.

Called a "hard-boiled poet" by National Public Radio's Maureen Corrigan and the "noir poet laureate" in the Huffington Post, REED FARREL COLEMAN is the author of twenty-one novels and novellas. He has been signed to do the next four books in Robert B. Parker's Jesse Stone series and by Putnam to begin a new series of his own. He is a three-time recipient of the Shamus Award and a three-time Edgar Award nominee in three different categories. He has also won the Audie, Macavity, Barry, and Anthony awards. He lives with his family on Long Island. For more information, visit www.reedcoleman.com.

Read the first two titles in the Gulliver Dowd mystery series

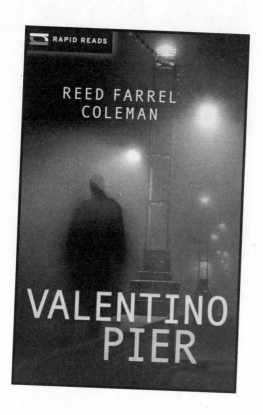

"Gulliver Dowd swaggers into the crime fiction world and takes his place with the great investigators. Smart, vulnerable, wounded, heartbreakingly hopeful, I just adore his company."

—*Louise Penny*

RAPID READS
WWW.RAPID-READS.COM